WHAT'S ALICE UP TO

HARLEY JESSUP

VIKING

To Ann, Katharine, Graham, and of course Alice

Published by the Penguin Group
Penguin Putnam Inc., 375 Hudson Street, New York, New York 10014, U.S.A.
Penguin Books Ltd, 27 Wrights Lane, London W8 5TZ, England
Penguin Books Australia Ltd, Ringwood, Victoria, Australia
Penguin Books Canada Ltd, 10 Alcorn Avenue, Toronto, Ontario, Canada M4V 3B2
Penguin Books (N.Z.) Ltd, 182–190 Wairau Road, Auckland 10, New Zealand

Penguin Books Ltd, Registered Offices: Harmondsworth, Middlesex, England

First published in 1997 by Viking, a member of Penguin Putnam Inc.

1 3 5 7 9 10 8 6 4 2

Copyright © Harley Jessup, 1997

LIBRARY OF CONGRESS CATALOGING-IN-PUBLICATION DATA
Jessup, Harley.
What's Alice up to? / Harley Jessup. p. cm.
Summary : A young girl acts mysteriously all day as she prepares a surprise for her dog.
ISBN 0-670-87396-9
[1 Dogs—Fiction. 2. Birthdays—Fiction. 3. Parties—Fiction.
4. Stories in rhyme.] I. Title.
PZ8.3.J553175Wh 1997 [E]—dc21 97-8822 CIP AC

Manufactured in China.   Set in Goudy.

What's Alice up to with that look in her eye?

What's Alice doing with her father's necktie?

Where's Alice going with that old worn-out rug?

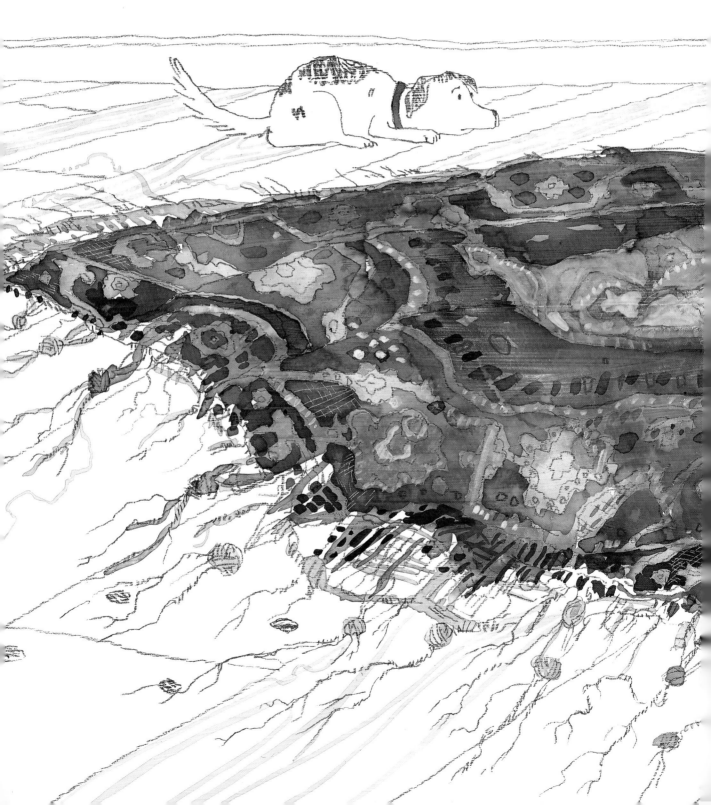

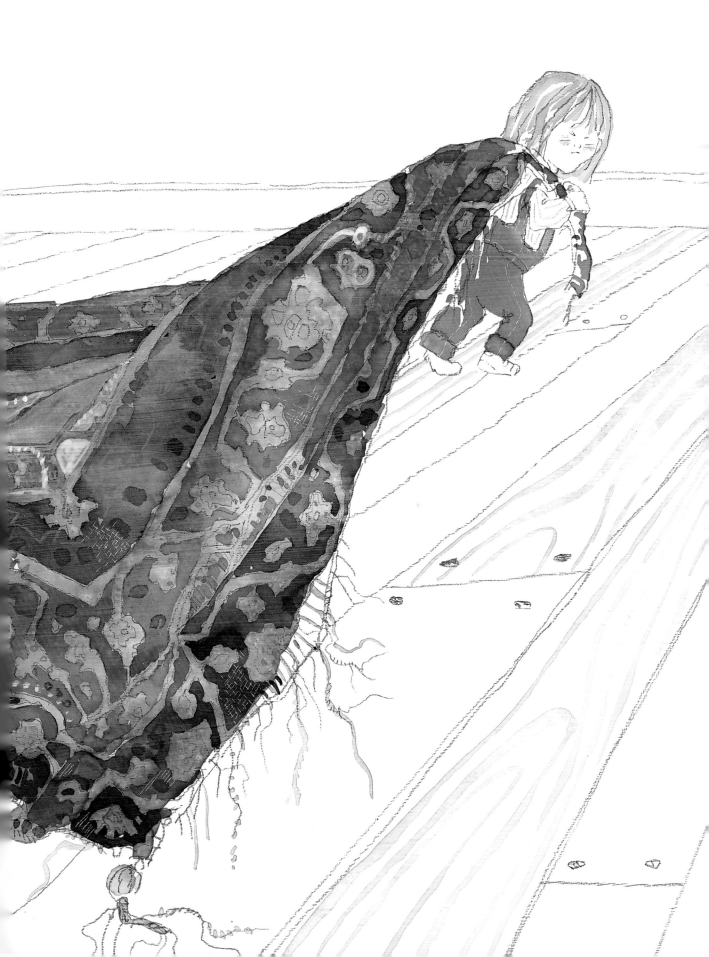

Just look, now she's crawling around like a slug!

Where's Alice pushing that comfy old chair?

Why is she painting the neighbor boy's hair?

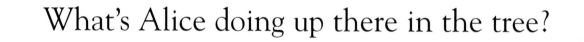

What's Alice doing up there in the tree?

She's not paying any attention to me.

She's hiding from me in her room all alone.

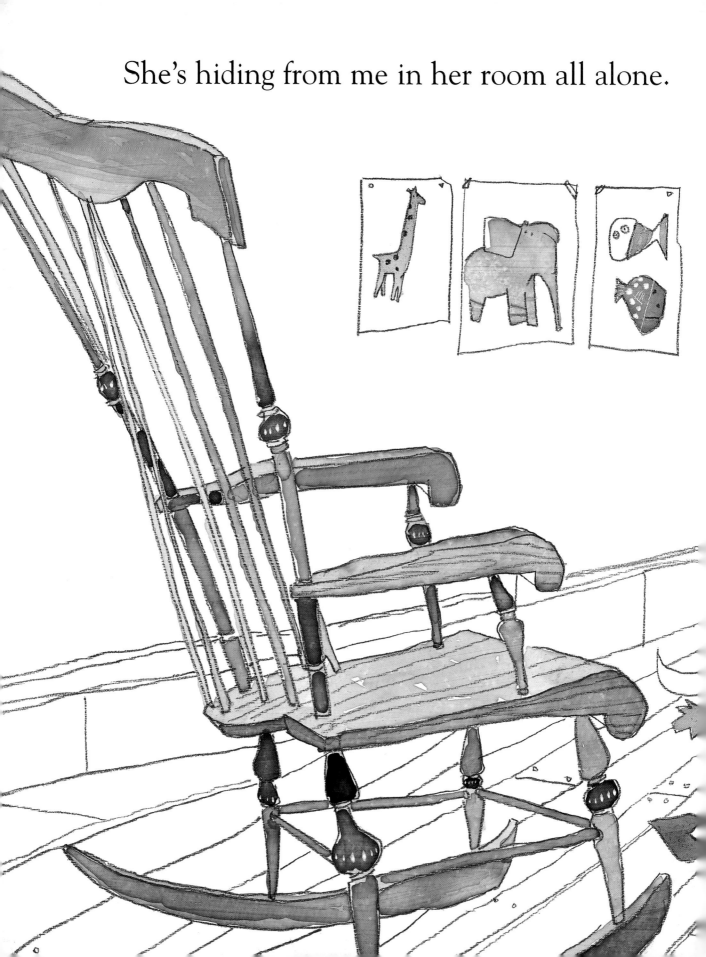

Where's Alice taking that lovely soup bone?

What's Alice doing with the cat in her arms?

Where's Alice going with that giant ant farm?

She shouldn't be taking those blueberry pies.

CHARLES
#048215

What's Alice up to?

It's my birthday surprise!